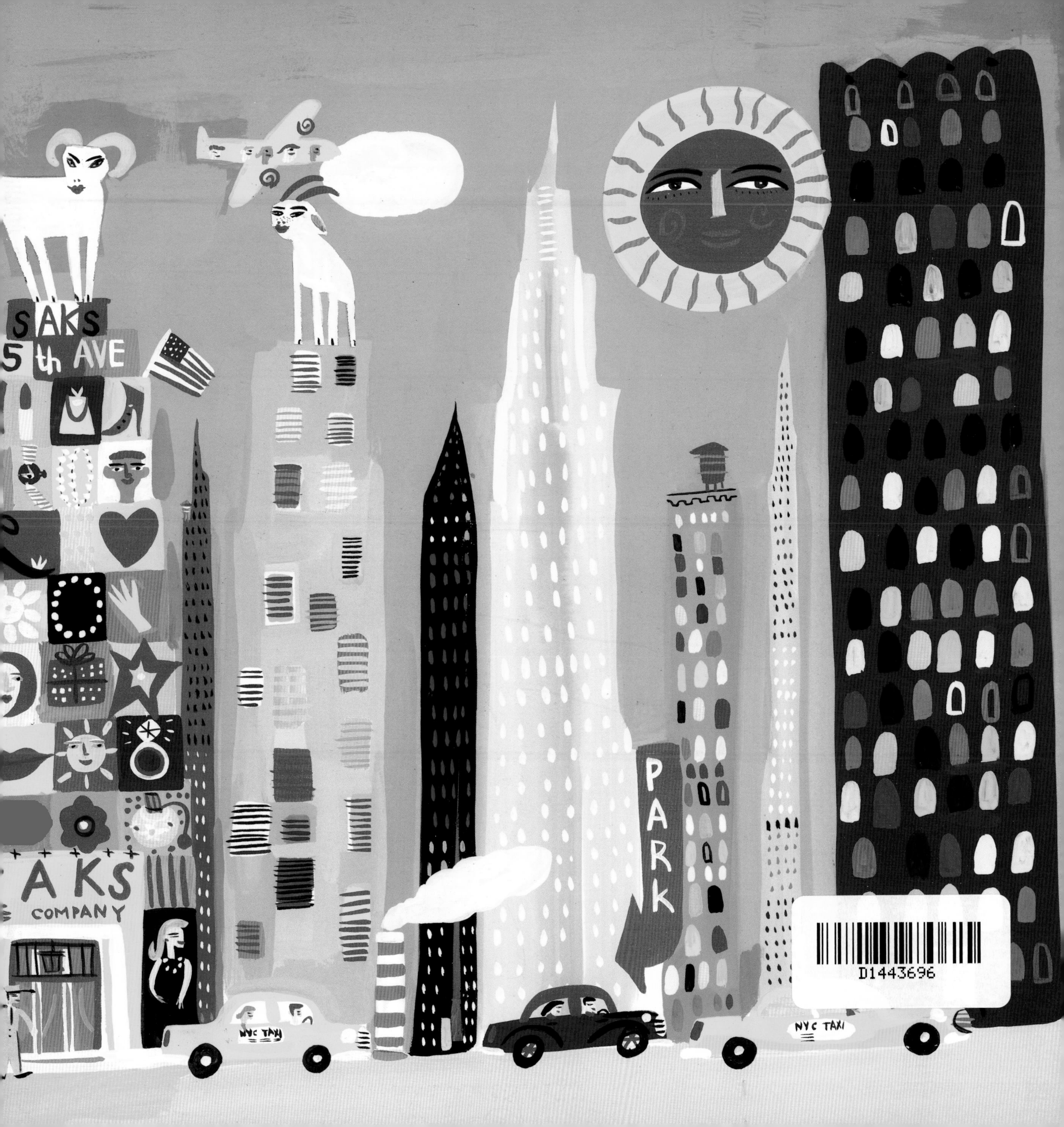
SAKS
5th AVE
PARK
AKS
COMPANY
NYC TAXI
NYC TAXI

D1443696

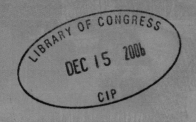

For
Honor and Christian
—TS

To Matthew
—CC

Cashmere If You Can

Text copyright © 2005 by Saks Fifth Avenue

Illustrations copyright © 2005 by Christopher Corr

Printed in the United State of America.

Library of Congress Cataloging-in-Publication Data is available.
ISBN-10: 0-06-089632-9 — ISBN-13: 978-0-06-089632-4

1 2 3 4 5 6 7 8 9 10
❖
First Edition

The story of Wawa Hohhot
as told to Terron Schaefer

CASHMERE IF YOU CAN

Illustrated by
Christopher Corr

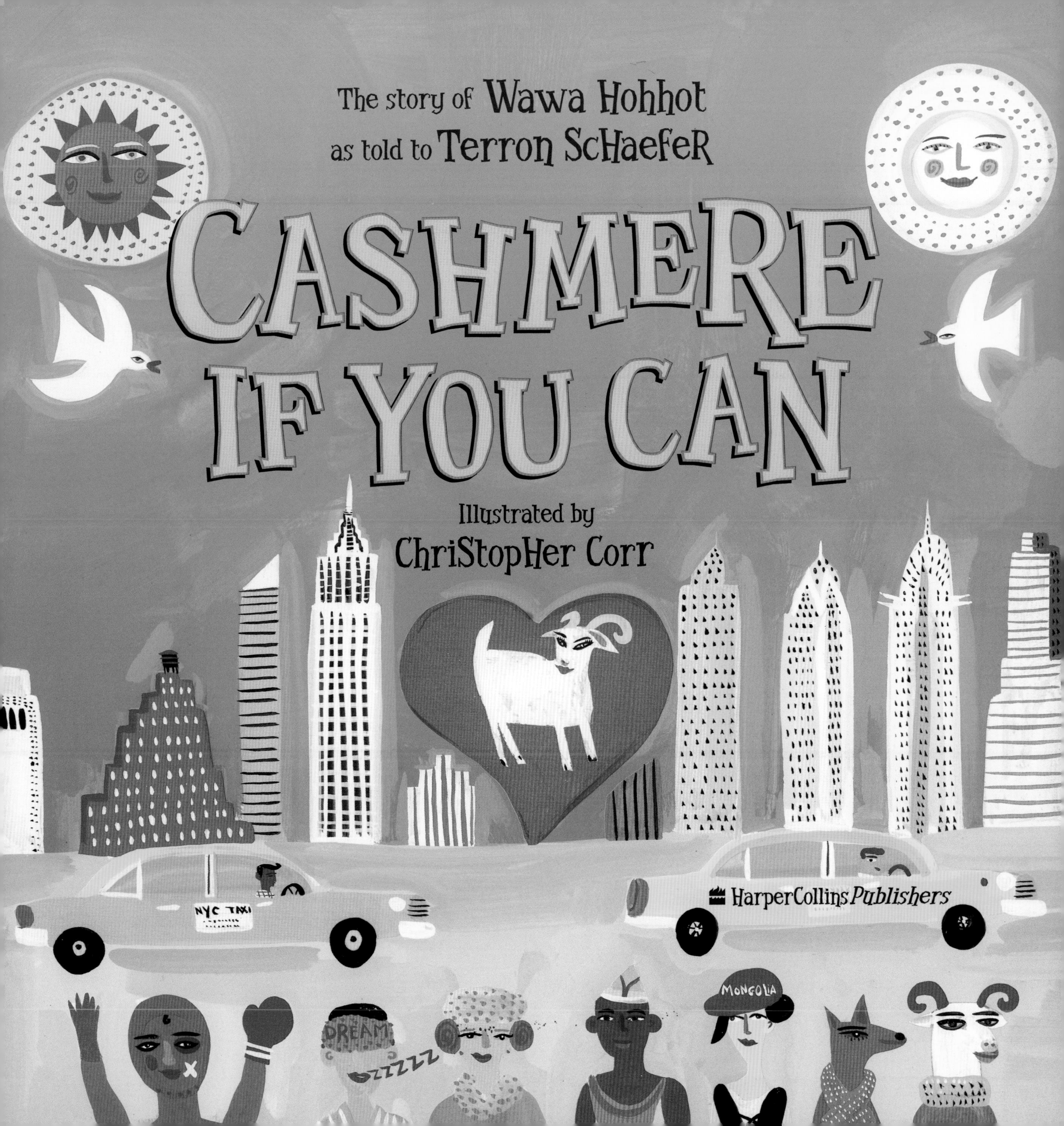
NYC TAXI
DREAM
ZZZZZ
MONGOLIA

HarperCollinsPublishers

Hi! My name is Wawa. Wawa Hohhot. I know, it sounds like something you'd say if you sat on a hot stove. It's a pretty ridiculous name for a person. But I'm not a person. I'M A CASHMERE GOAT.

I live in MONGOLIA in a little town called New Rock City. New Rock, New Rock. THE BIG GRAVEL.

If you can make it here . . . YOU'RE A GOAT.

One day, a tourist left behind the Sunday *Gotham Times* from NEW YORK. My family just devoured it. Mom ate the theater section. My little brother, Hauhau, GOBBLED up sports. My dad tried to swallow the editorials.

There was one section left for me—
THE STYLE SECTION.

I read it over and over, thinking about the **GLAMOROUS** lives the models must lead. I didn't eat a bit of it. Except the perfume samples, to keep my breath fresh.

Then another tourist left a camera behind. I had Hauhau take photos of me in my **BEST MODELING POSES.**

He gave me the **nicest** compliment a little brother ever gave a sister: "You don't look half ugly." I was so flattered! I mailed the pictures off to SAKS FIFTH AVENUE.

A few days later
I got a **LETTER!**

AIR MAIL

Miss Hohhot

Dear Miss Hohhot,

I've never seen a woman look so natural in a cashmere outfit. It is almost like a second skin on you.

HOLY FLANKS AND FETLOCKS!
He didn't know I was a goat! He thought I was a GIRL! A girl girl! And I wasn't about to tell him otherwise—especially after I read the next part:

I would love you to model in our upcoming Wild About Cashmere fashion show. I am enclosing plane tickets for you and your family.

Sincerely,
Mr. Saks

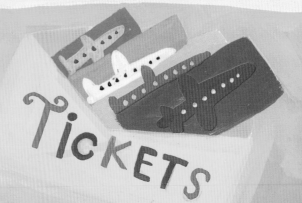

TiCKETS

We were so excited, and what a trip!
We ate the SEAT CUSHIONS
and the
OXYGEN MASKS
and the
HEADPHONES....

We ate everything on the plane
but the in-flight meal.
It was cannelloni,
AND IT WAS TERRIBLE.

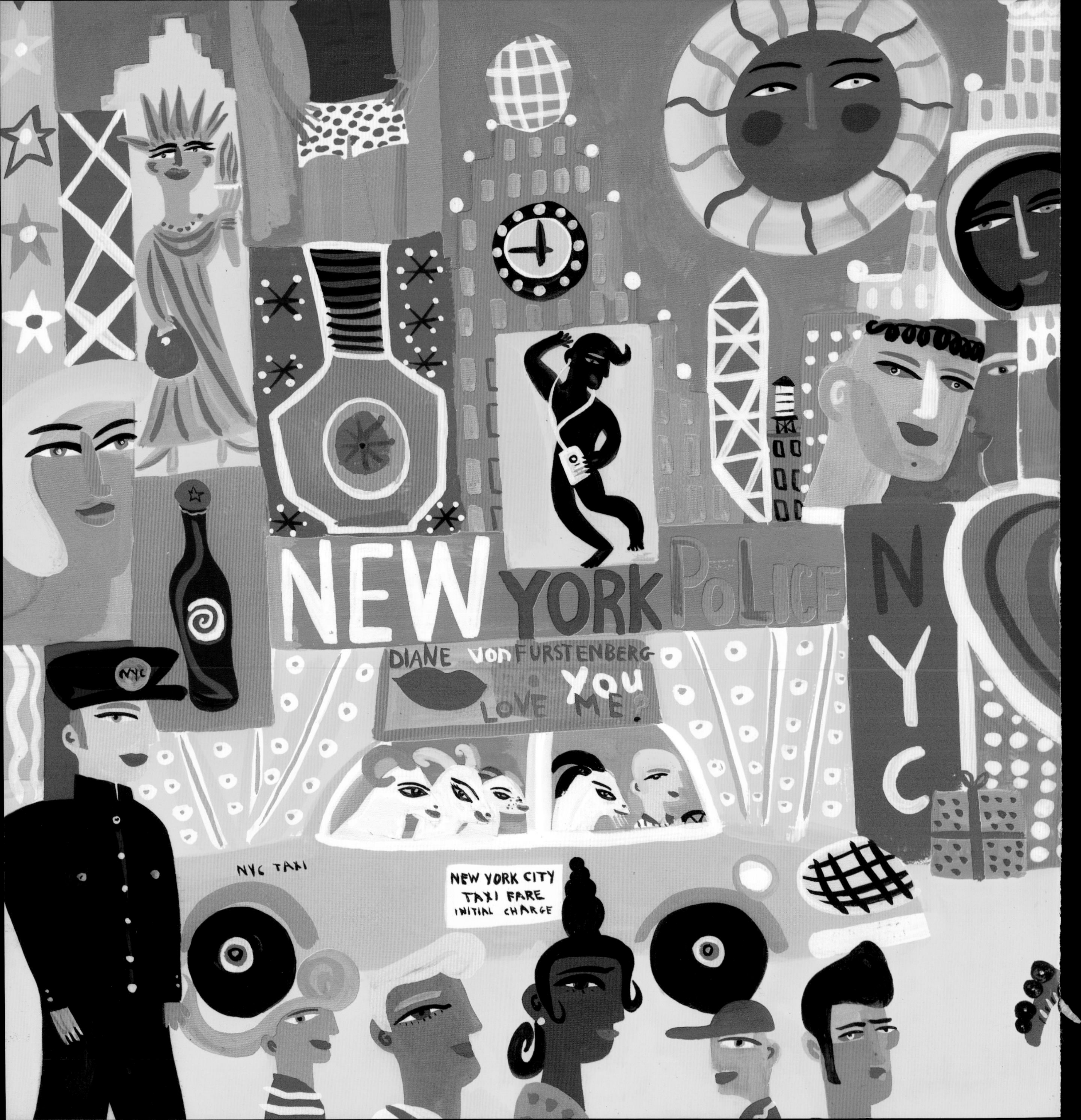
NEW YORK POLICE
NYC
DIANE von FURSTENBERG
LOVE YOU ME?
NYC
NYC TAXI
NEW YORK CITY
TAXI FARE
INITIAL CHARGE

TIMES SQUARE IS AN ELECTRIC ISLAND

PARK

JIMMY CHEW

WOW

KISS ME NOW

We got to New York and met a cab driver named Mr. Czprzomxyzptlk.

When he heard this was our first trip to the city, he gave us a **SPECIAL RATE:** JFK to Manhattan for $728. Plus tip.

What a nice man.

Five hours later, ... we got to **SAKS**.
It was the most beautiful place I'd ever seen.
"I thought there'd be more sacks," grumbled my dad.
It was getting late. I still had to prepare for the FASHION
SHOW. I asked my family not to come with me:
"If they know I'm a goat, they'll **NEVER** let me be a model."

My parents looked sad, but they understood.
"Don't worry, Wawa. We can have fun
exploring the city!" said my dad.
"I just hope we don't look WEIRD," said Hauhau.
They left just in time.

MR. SAKS appeared and whisked me into the store, where employees were waiting to help me get ready for the FASHION SHOW.

FIRST STOP: the shoe department for high heels. I wear a size two on my left feet, size six on the right. This helps me stand on hillsides.

NEXT,

the famous
RED DOOR SALON,
where two men trimmed,
teased, streaked, and blew out
my CASHMERE.

"She doesn't look like
a typical model," said
Jean-Claude.

"Agree," said Claude-Jean.
"She looks like . . . she looks
like . . ."

Oh, no! My secret was
about to be revealed!

"She looks like
Holly Goat Lightly!"
said Jean-Claude.

"Agree," said Claude-Jean.

Then I went to the perfume department,
where two women sprayed me.
And sprayed me.
And
sprayed
me.

"For some reason,
she smells a little . . . goat-y," said one.
"Keep spraying," said the other.

The last step was makeup. Rouge, lipstick, mascara, pancake, mousse—my stomach growled.

I COULD HAVE EATEN IT ALL.

I was famished, but I was too nervous to eat.

The last thing I'd eaten was the in-flight MAGAZINE on the plane.

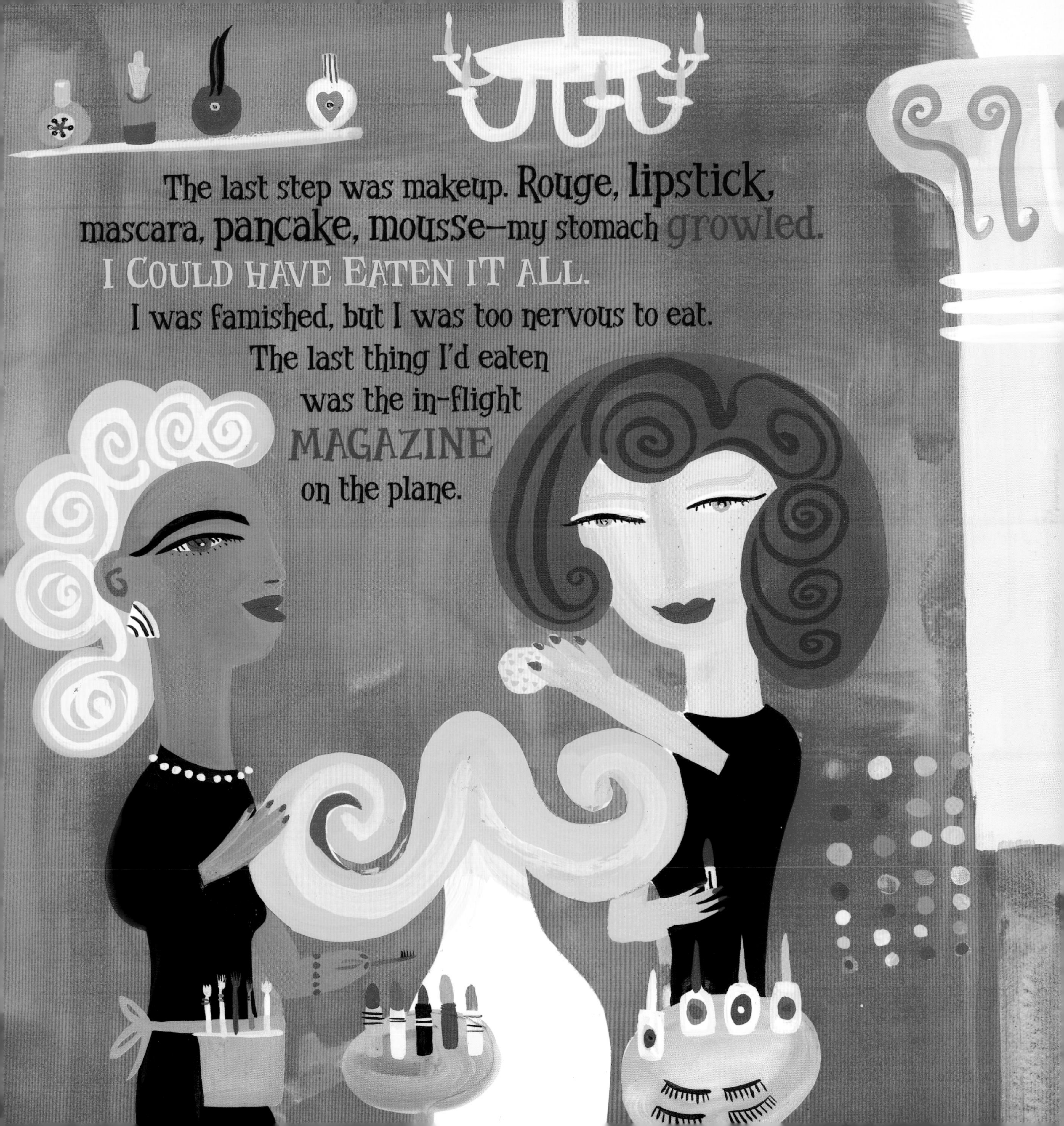

Meanwhile,
my mom, dad, and brother were having their
own adventures in the city.
Little Hauhau fell asleep on the SUBWAY. And when
he woke up, he was covered with graffiti.

He walked into an art supply store in **SOHO**, wiped his face on one canvas, shook the paint off his body onto another one . . .

. . . and in the process, created **TWO** masterpieces.

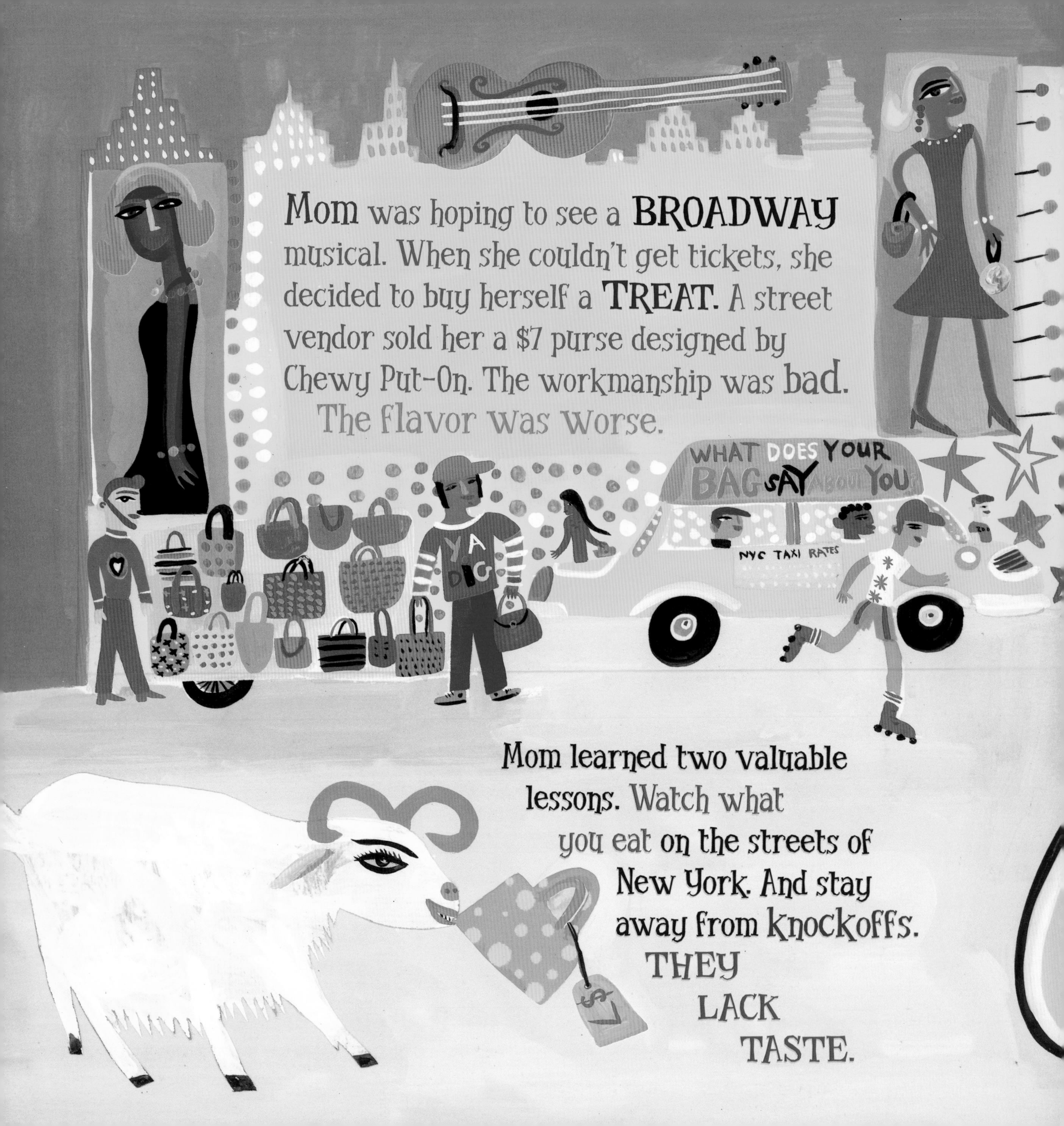
WHAT DOES YOUR BAG SAY ABOUT YOU?
NYC TAXI RATES
YA DIG

Mom was hoping to see a **BROADWAY** musical. When she couldn't get tickets, she decided to buy herself a **TREAT**. A street vendor sold her a $7 purse designed by Chewy Put-On. The workmanship was bad.
The flavor was worse.

Mom learned two valuable lessons. Watch what you eat on the streets of New York. And stay away from knockoffs.
THEY
LACK
TASTE.

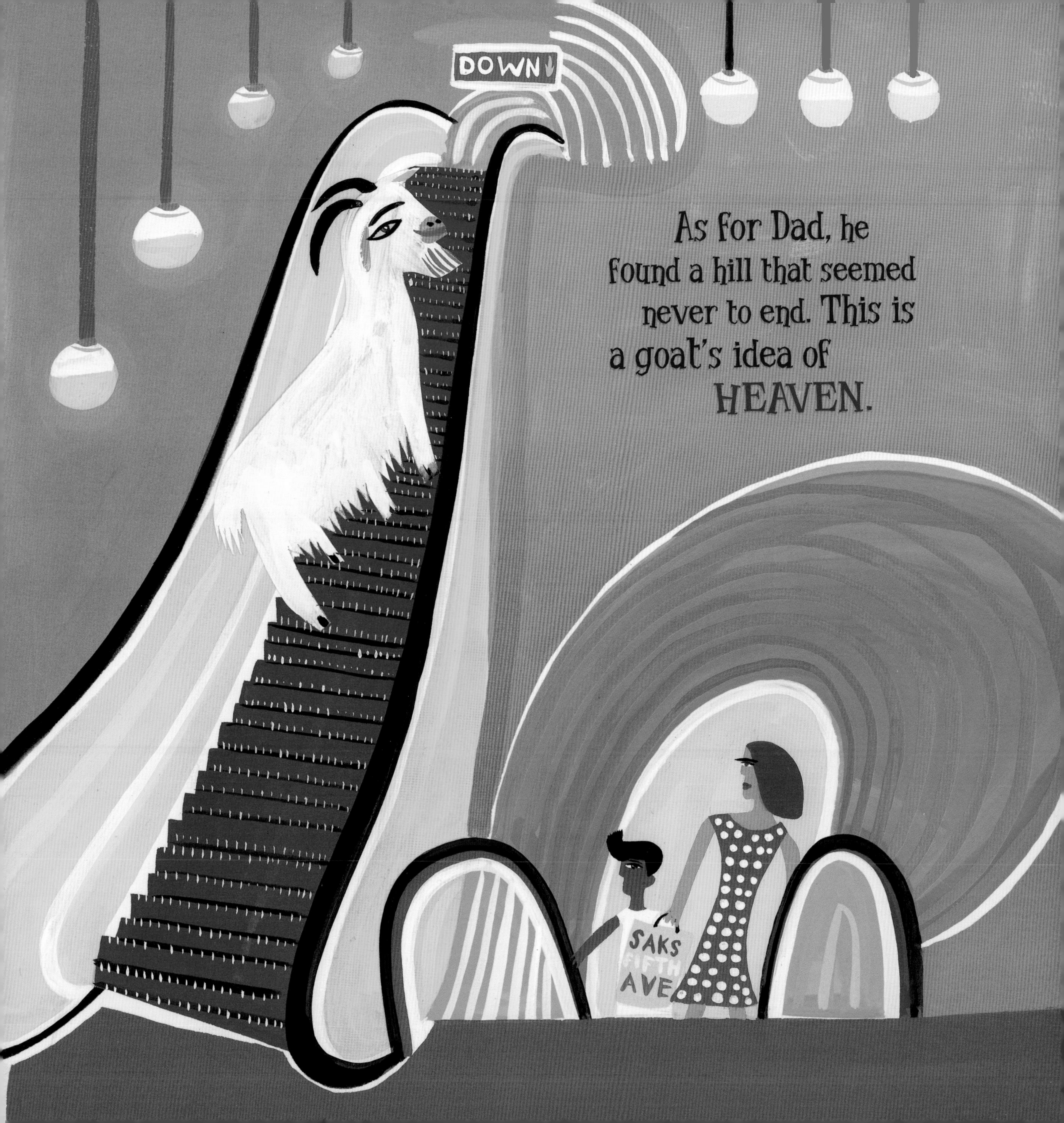
DOWN
SAKS
FIFTH
AVE

As for Dad, he found a hill that seemed never to end. This is a goat's idea of HEAVEN.

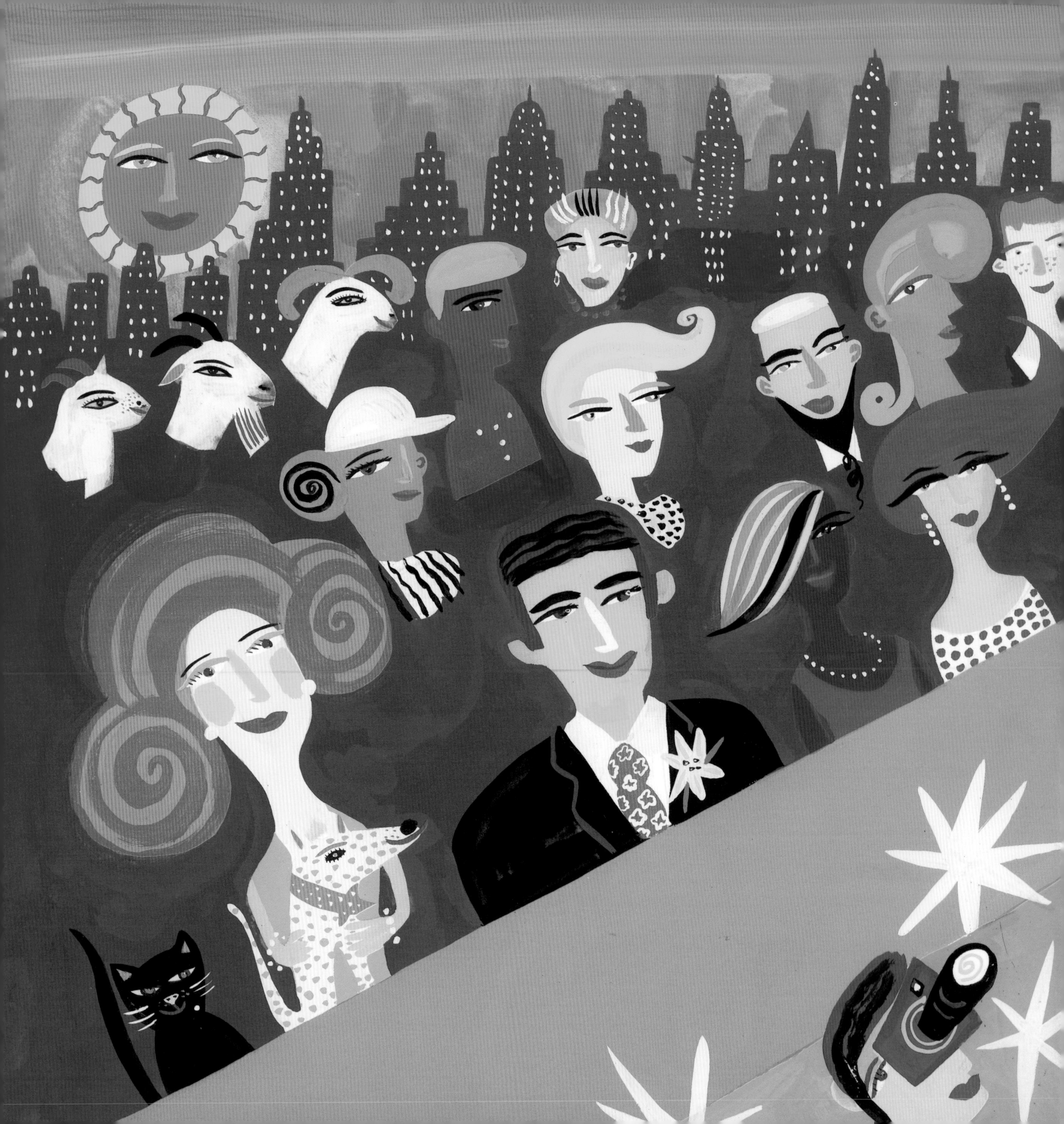

Up on the roof of Saks, just as the
sun was setting, the fashion show began.
EVERYONE WAS THERE.
Celebrities, designers, the whole city.
In the back row, trying not to be seen,
was my family; and in the front row,
smiling proudly, was MR. SAKS.

I was a model now. I was proud. I was beautiful.
But mostly, I was starving. As I strutted down the
catwalk, I couldn't take my eyes off the flowers on
Mr. Saks' lapel. THEY LOOKED SO YUMMY!
Well, I just lost it. I leapt off the stage and
onto Mr. Saks. I ate that delicious flower
and a good deal of his suit, too.

"HELP!"
cried Mr. Saks.
"My supermodel . . .
is a goat!"
Saks security, the
best dressed in the
business, raced to
the rooftop. I
scampered with
goat-like grace to the
top of the chimney.

As the crowd gathered around me, I knew that my career as a model was over. "I'm sorry I tried to fool you all," I cried. "I'm just a goat. We make beautiful cashmere and our cheese isn't bad either. I should be what I was meant to be, and take pride in who I am."

Everyone was silent. Then Mr. Saks began to applaud. The crowd joined in! My dad whistled, my mom cried, and Hauhau proclaimed,

"Hey! That's my sister!"

A designer stepped forward and held up a hand for silence. "I applaud this girl's bravery. For I too have a secret. I started out as a kid growing up on a farm. I am Jean Paul Goatier . . . **AND I AM A GOAT!"**

"I'M A DOG!" barked Yves Saint Bernard.

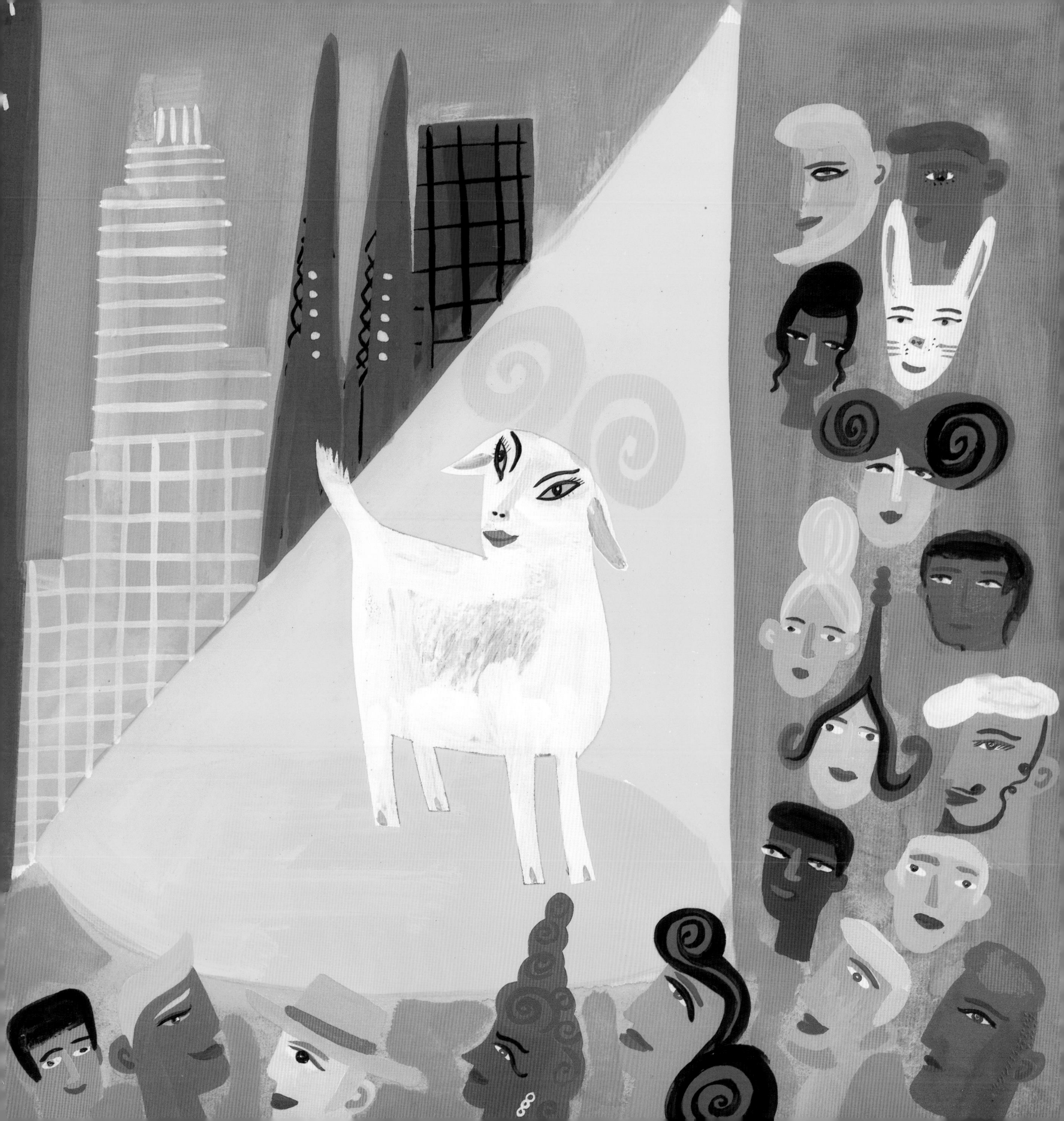

Well, I bet YOU didn't know that most fashion designers are actually ANIMALS.

Billy Goat Blass

Giorgio Farmani

D&G&O&A&T

And they all **HIRED ME** to model their clothes!

Cheese Van Noten

Comme des Chèvres

Fursace

The Hohhot family is **LOVING LIFE** in the city. Hauhau sells a lot of paintings.

BEST MUSICAL

GOATS

And Mom wrote a **BROADWAY SHOW!**

GO GOAT

GOATS WINNER 8 TONY AWARDS

THE SOLOMON R. GUGGENHEIM MUSEUM

Even Dad found a job.

Manolo Blaahnik!

TAXI FARE

As for me—well, I'm now Saks' TOP MODEL!

NY TIMES

HO HHOT!

HoT!   HoT!

We have a wonderful home, right on the roof of SAKS FIFTH AVENUE. Drop by and see us next time you're IN THE STORE. New York City. New York, New York. THE BIG APPLE.

If you can make it here . . . YOU'RE A GOAT.